First published in the UK by Sweet Cherry Publishing Limited, 2024
Unit 36, Vulcan House, Vulcan Road,
Leicester, LE5 3EF, United Kingdom

Sweet Cherry Europe (Europe address)
Nauschgasse 4/3/2 POB 1017
Vienna, WI 1220, Austria

2 4 6 8 10 9 7 5 3 1

ISBN: 978-1-80263-151-7

Football Rising Stars: Aitana Bonmatí

© Sweet Cherry Publishing Limited, 2024

Text by Harry Meredith
Illustrations by Sophie Jones

All rights reserved. No part of this publication may be reproduced or utilised in any form or by any means, electronic or mechanical, including photocopying, recording, or using any information storage and retrieval system, without prior permission in writing from the publisher.

The right of Harry Meredith to be identified as the author of this work has been asserted by them in accordance with the Copyright, Designs and Patents Act 1988.

www.sweetcherrypublishing.com

Printed and bound in Turkey

AITANA BONMATÍ
THE UNOFFICIAL STORY

Written by
HARRY MEREDITH

Sweet Cherry

CONTENTS

1.	Copa de la Reina	7
2.	Sant Pere de Ribes	19
3.	Fierce & Fearless	26
4.	Juvenile-Cadets	31
5.	Around the World	37
6.	Barcelona B	47
7.	The Waiting Game	51
8.	Captain Bonmatí	60
9.	La Blaugrana	74
10.	National Team	81
11.	Liga F	96
12.	The Treble	100
13.	Euro 2022	110
14.	Campiones!	120

COPA DE LA REINA

On the 13th of February 2021, the Barcelona team walked out onto the pitch in the La Rosaleda stadium, in Málaga, to an eerie silence. This wasn't because they didn't have any fans – far from it! Barcelona were one of the most popular football clubs in the world. Usually, thousands of fans would be cheering for them as they made their way onto the pitch for a clash in the final of the Copa de la Reina, an important Spanish domestic cup. But this time, fans were not allowed to watch football matches in stadiums as a precaution against the COVID-19 pandemic. It was an extraordinary time, almost the whole world had gone into lockdown, and it meant football fans had to watch their beloved matches from afar, on TVs, instead

✦ AITANA BONMATÍ ✦

of being able to cheer on their team in person.

Barcelona's opponents were a team known at the time as EDF Logroño. (They have since been renamed DUX Logroño.) They were a team on the rise and had recently been promoted to the top division in Spain. EDF Logroño had never reached the final of this competition before and they were determined to win. But Barcelona were standing in their way. Barcelona were one of the giants of Spanish football and wanted to win the cup just as badly as their opponents. Without the fans to cheer them on and give them an all-important boost, Barcelona knew their players would have to dig deep, come together as a team and work as hard as they could to bring the cup home.

Aitana Bonmatí, a player who was Barcelona through-and-through, knew the team would be relying heavily on her. She was one of the younger players at only twenty-three years old, but she was a vital part of Barcelona's midfield. Aitana was known to be a powerful, technical

AITANA BONMATÍ

and determined player who always gave her all on the pitch. She knew the team were facing unusual circumstances in this match and was determined to step up and play her part. Like the rest of her team, she wanted to make sure that they all took the match seriously and showed the grit and heart necessary to win the competition.

The beginning of the match was tough, with neither side able to find the back of the net. Barcelona were determined to keep trying, and eventually created the perfect opportunity for themselves towards the end of the first half. They were awarded a penalty, and Alexia Putellas stepped forward to take it. Aitana watched from outside the box as her teammate ran up to strike the ball. Putellas kicked the ball into the right-hand corner with her left foot. Barcelona held their breath as the opposition goalkeeper tried and failed to stop the ball from hitting the back of the net. Aitana ran over  to Putellas with the rest of the team. As they came together for a group hug in

★ AITANA BONMATÍ ★

the penalty box, they knew there was no time to relax. To win the match, they needed to keep up the pressure and push for more.

Minutes later, Aitana made a darting run into the opposition's half. She knew the clock was ticking, and the half-time whistle fast approaching, but she wasn't going to let anyone, or anything, get in her way. Aitana ran past the defenders and found herself on the edge of the box. She looked up towards the goal, working out where to place her shot, then fired the ball.

The thwack of her shot echoed around the silent stadium. The ball flew into the top right corner of the net and Barcelona had another goal! In the space of only a few minutes the team had turned a 0-0 scoreline into a 2-0 lead. Aitana and the team celebrated once more, but they knew the game was far from over. They headed into their dressing rooms determined to come back out and win the match. They were very aware that there was still an entire half of football to be played. Barcelona could not afford to be complacent, and every single player needed to bring the same intensity and desire into the second half. And Aitana was going to make sure that was the case.

Logroño tried their best to get past the Barcelona defence, but it was proving difficult. Aitana and the rest of their players had found their rhythm and there was no stopping Barcelona when the players were feeling this confident. Everyone who watched the match could see how much they were enjoying themselves.

In the 60th minute, Jenni Hermoso rose highest in the box to meet a driven cross and effortlessly headed the ball into the back of the net. Barcelona were now in the lead by 3-0.

The team held onto this scoreline for the remaining thirty minutes. Finally, the referee blew the whistle at full time and Barcelona's celebrations began. They had done it; they were the champions of the Copa de la Reina once again. They had triumphed and added yet another trophy to the club's ever-growing trophy cabinet.

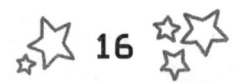

★ AITANA BONMATÍ ★

Because of the precautions put in place due to COVID-19, Barcelona's captain, Vicky Losada, was the only player allowed to enter the stands to collect the trophy. Aitana and the rest of her teammates had to wait on the pitch. The players sang and cheered as their captain accepted the trophy from a small group of delegates wearing face masks and spaced carefully apart to stop any possible infection from spreading. Losada accepted the trophy, then rushed down to the pitch to continue celebrating with her team.

After the match Aitana was named as the MVP, which is an award given to the most valuable player on the pitch for their effort and performance. Aitana was a star, and a Catalonian whose blood ran garnet and blue – Barcelona's team colours.

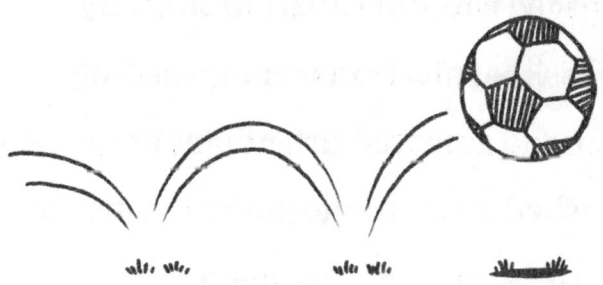

SANT PERE DE RIBES

Aitana Bonmatí was born a fighter. Almost from her first breath, she was taught to stand up for what is right and what she believed in. Aitana was born on the 18th of January 1998 to two loving and caring parents, Vicent Conca and Rosa Bonmatí

Guidonet. Her parents were determined to raise their only child in a fair and equal society, away from what they saw as outdated Spanish traditions.

At this time in Spain, children usually had two surnames. The first was always their father's surname and the second their mother's. But Aitana's parents believed that this made women seem less important than men. They desperately wanted this to change and for their daughter to bear her mother's surname first. But Spanish law meant they had to

AITANA BONMATÍ

follow this custom, so for the first two years of her life, she was known as Aitana Conca Bonmatí.

Aitana's parents fought for this rule to change. And finally, a new law was passed allowing children to bear the surname of their mother first. Aitana was one of the first children in her country to take her mother's surname first. From that day onwards, she was known as Aitana Bonmatí Conca.

Aitana grew up in a small and charming town known as Sant Pere de Ribes in the province of Barcelona, a famous and proud city within the

Catalonian region of Spain. Sant Pere de Ribes was known for its impressive 12th century castle, but there wasn't much to do for the children who lived there. Aitana used to head out with the neighbourhood kids and play game after game of basketball. But when she was seven, she decided she wanted to try football instead. The first time she kicked a ball, Aitana knew she'd found her passion and she was determined to keep playing.

One day at school, Aitana summoned the courage to ask the boys if she could play football with them in the playground. This itself was a small act of rebellion because, back then, many people still believed that football was a boys' sport. Thankfully this old-fashioned attitude was starting to change, but there were still people who hung on to it.

The boys huddled up to discuss Aitana's request. Some of them thought she was way too small and wouldn't be able to keep up, but in the end Aitana was allowed to join in. Aitana threw herself into the game, practising her passing, shooting and tackling, and soon she was a fixture in the playground matches. It wasn't always easy for Aitana. Some of the boys would go in for aggressive tackles or refuse to pass to her just because she was a girl. But Aitana  was determined to stand up for herself. If someone pushed her, she pushed them back. And if someone didn't pass to her, she simply ignored them and let her football skills do the talking. Before long, everyone knew that if they wanted to be on the winning team, they should pass the ball to Aitana.

AITANA BONMATÍ

It wasn't long before Aitana's skills outgrew just playing football in the playground. She longed to develop as a player, and believed she was ready to test her abilities against better players and in competitive matches that mattered. Aitana's parents were more than happy to support their daughter in living up to her potential. It was decided. Aitana was going to look for a football team to join.

3
FIERCE & FEARLESS

There was one problem with Aitana's search for a club to join. There weren't any suitable girls-only teams nearby. This meant Aitana would have to join a mixed team of boys and girls playing competitive football matches together. It also meant

AITANA BONMATÍ

Aitana would face more pressure and judgement than if she had joined a girls' team, but she wasn't going to let anything get in her way.

Aitana joined a local team known as CD Ribes. She couldn't wait to get started. It wasn't just a place for her to learn and develop with other players, it was an opportunity for Aitana to have some fun. This was a chance for her to make new friends and fill her time with laughter, adventures and most importantly, football!

During her four years at CD Ribes, Aitana usually played on teams mostly made up of boys. Sometimes she would be the only girl on the team, but she wasn't fazed by this at all. The boys who played with her soon realised that they had an incredible player amongst them. It was in this tough environment that Aitana developed her close control and strength. She quickly learnt how to protect the ball from oncoming defenders, who were often much larger than her, and she rarely let them steal the ball. Aitana had discovered that her small frame and low centre of gravity was far from a weakness, but an ability that she could use to her advantage.

When Aitana turned eleven, she was offered a new challenge – to join a team known as CF Cubelles. Yet again, she was able to challenge and test her skills and continue to develop. But within two years, it was obvious that Aitana was outplaying everyone else there. She wasn't just the team's top player; she was a girl who could make it to the very top of the football world. To anyone who had seen her play, it came as no surprise when Aitana was given an opportunity that millions of football players across the world dreamed of. She was invited to train and learn at Barcelona FC – an academy that had developed countless skilled, mesmerising and world-class footballers. *Perhaps*, Aitana thought, *if I train hard enough, maybe, just maybe I could add my name to that list.*

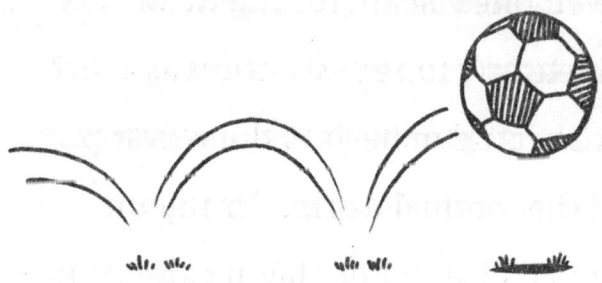

JUVENILE-CADETS

Barcelona's academy is one of the most famous in the world of football. It's a melting pot for hundreds of talented young players desperate to make it into the Barcelona first team. The academy players are taught a very distinct style that has become known as tiki-taka football. This style of play revolves entirely around keeping possession of the ball. Players torment their opposition, bypassing them with rapid-fire passes and constant movement. It's an incredibly fluid and, at times, untouchable style of football.

Aitana started at the academy at the age of thirteen and immediately took to the Barcelona style of football like she had played it all her life. She had grown up as a proud Catalonian and this style of football was in her blood. Aitana lived and breathed

AITANA BONMATÍ

Barcelona. She had watched some of her footballing idols such as Lionel Messi, Andrés Iniesta and Xavi show off their tiki-taka skills. And she had joined in with the roar of the fans at Camp Nou, Barcelona's stadium, as they watched the players turning football into art.

Out of all the players, Xavi was her idol. The small midfielder was rarely seen losing possession of the ball. Aitana would watch him closely, studying the way he played. She admired how well Xavi could read the game and wanted more than anything to be able to do the same.

Aitana was selected to train with the part of the Barcelona academy structure known as the Juvenile-Cadets. Attending the frequent training and matches wasn't always easy for Aitana. It was a tedious two-hour journey on public transport from her school to Barcelona FC. These long journeys were tiring and left Aitana with little to no time to do anything else apart from football and school. But it was a sacrifice that Aitana was only too happy to make. All she wanted was to keep learning, playing and developing alongside some of the best players in the world.

It wasn't long before Aitana played an important role in helping her team succeed. They won their respective league and performed well in a cup competition called the Copa Catalunya, making it through to the final. Barcelona and Sant Gabriel battled each other on the pitch, both determined to win. In the end, the match went to extra time and was decided by penalties. Aitana scored a penalty, but Barcelona lost the shoot-out 4-2 to Sant Gabriel.

The coaches at Barcelona had noticed Aitana's impressive performances. It was clear that she had everything it took – and more – to be a Barcelona player. Aitana's talent and skill was obvious to anyone who saw her play, so it wasn't a surprise that she was also on the Spanish national team's radar. A youth tournament was fast approaching, and the national coaches would need to pick which players to take with them.

5
AROUND THE WORLD

At fifteen years old, Aitana was too young to join the women's national team, but the coaches wanted to make sure that her talent didn't go to waste, and she was invited to join one of the youth teams. Football teams have multiple year groups for football players, in the same way schools have year groups. This ensures that the best talent in the country learn and develop alongside their peers. It also means that young players learn their country's style of play and prepare for life as an international footballer.

Aitana was ready to burst with excitement at the opportunity in front of her, but there was one big problem. Aitana was scared of flying. The thought of getting on a plane and travelling at hundreds of miles an hour through the clouds filled her with fear. The rational part of her knew that flying was a very safe way to travel, but she was still terrified. Despite her fear, her mind was made up. She knew she had been offered the opportunity of a lifetime. There was no way that she was going to let her anxiety get in the way of her future. It was this single-mindedness that made Aitana who she was, on and off the pitch.

Aitana played with the Spain under 17 squad in two tournaments that year, representing her country in the U17 Euros and the U17 World Cup. Spain didn't win either competition,

but they were still incredibly valuable experiences for Aitana. The matches gave her the chance to play against many different styles of football. As well as the opportunity to play with and against the very best female football players across the world.

Aitana's talent definitely made an impression on the national team coaches. One year later, in 2015, Aitana was invited back to compete with the Spain U17 side. This time, she would be playing in the

★ AITANA BONMATÍ ★

2015 Women's Championship being held in Iceland. Every year, eight teams from Europe took part in the tournament. It meant Aitana had to get on a plane again and she was still a very nervous flyer. As the plane took off, instead of worrying, she closed her eyes and imagined the football pitch awaiting her in Iceland. Throughout the flight, Aitana stayed in her imaginary football bubble, thinking of the goals and the pitch, and dreamt about what it would feel like to actually win the competition.

Spain had been drawn in Group A and would play against England, Germany and Iceland. Their first match was against England, and it ended as a 1-1 draw. In the second match, Spain defeated Germany 4-0. Aitana even got herself on the score sheet with an 84th minute goal. And they continued as they meant to go on, by winning their third match against Iceland 0-2, making it through to the knock-out stages.

As the tournament only had eight teams, Spain's first knock-out match

was the semi-final. Spain had to get past France if they were going to reach the final. Spain and France fought against one another in a tight fixture that ended 1-1. This meant that the match had to be decided by penalties. Each side needed five players to take a penalty and Aitana volunteered for Spain. She knew she had what it took to carry out a penalty under pressure. And Aitana's confidence in herself wasn't misplaced. The teenager scored her penalty, helping Spain to a 4-3 victory. They were through to the final where they would face Switzerland for the right to be crowned tournament champions.

Aitana knew her team could do it. Spain were ready to fight. And fight they did. Spain took the lead early in the match and went on to comfortably win 5-2. Aitana played

a vital role in the centre of the pitch, controlling the game and making pass after pass that kept her opponents firmly on the back foot. When the final whistle went, the Spanish players and coaches jumped in the air.

★ AITANA BONMATÍ ★

They had won the Women's Championship trophy. Aitana danced, pumped her fists in the air and enjoyed every single moment of the team's triumph. She loved this feeling; it was like nothing she had ever felt before. She was a winner, and as far as she was concerned, she had only just got started.

In recognition of her hard work, Aitana was named as one of the players of the tournament. She was no longer Barcelona's secret superstar. She had shown her brilliance on an international stage and had caught the attention of the footballing world.

BARCELONA B

Some of Europe's biggest football clubs have two secondary teams: a B team and a reserve team. Essentially, a reserve team is a squad filled with players who, although talented, aren't quite ready for the main team. Almost all clubs have a reserve team, but only a handful have a B team. The difference is that a B team competes in a competitive league structure a division or two below the main team, while reserve squads usually play in leagues behind closed doors.

The coaches had been seriously impressed by Aitana and decided it was now time for her to step up to Barcelona B. Aitana couldn't hide her excitement. She would be playing competitive matches in games that truly mattered in the Segunda Division, the second tier of women's

AITANA BONMATÍ

football in Spain. She knew she didn't have an easy ride ahead. Aitana would have to prove herself if she was going to achieve her childhood dream of making it all the way to the Barcelona first team.

It took Aitana some time to settle into her club, but soon she was an unstoppable force, passing each and every test with flying colours. Thanks to her goals – she scored fourteen in one season – Barcelona B went on to win the Segunda Division for the first time in the club's history. Scoring that many goals would be an achievement for a striker let alone a midfielder. Aitana had shown that she was far more than a midfield maestro, she was a lethal attacking midfielder who could cause serious damage to the defence of any team that dared to go up against her.

But at the end of the 2015/2016 campaign, the coaches made a decision that would affect Aitana's future forever.

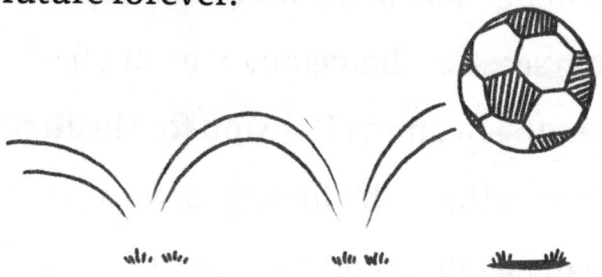

THE WAITING GAME

To Aitana's delight, she was promoted to the Barcelona first team. She was now part of the historic team that competed in the top division of football in Spain. She would also be taking part in the Champions League and numerous domestic cup competitions. But this was no time for Aitana to relax or take it easy. She had earned herself a spot in the squad, but it would take time for her to make her way onto the pitch.

As one of the best women's football teams in the world, Barcelona's team was brimming with talent. In 2016, the year that Aitana made the step up, the club was bursting with football stars. There was the talented striker Hermoso, the efficient midfielder Losada and the  emerging star Alexia Putellas. In the 2015/2016 campaign,

AITANA BONMATÍ

Barcelona had one of their worst seasons to date. They had failed to win the league title and lost the final of the Copa de la Reina. While finishing second and making it to the final of the national cup competition would be a cause for celebration for most teams, that wasn't the case for Barcelona. This was a team that expected to triumph, a side that demanded perfection. Anything less was seen as a failure.

So, there was real pressure on the team to perform during the 2016/2017 campaign. It meant that experienced players were picked to play rather than taking a risk on talented youngsters. Having been a starter for the majority of her footballing career, this was difficult for Aitana to deal with. She had gone from being one of the first names on the team sheet to a player who didn't always even make it onto the bench. Aitana tried her best not to be impatient. She couldn't change if she was picked or not, but she could control her attitude, how hard she worked on the training pitch, and how eager she was to learn and

AITANA BONMATÍ

develop. It was more important than ever for Aitana to keep pushing herself forward and make the most of any opportunity that came her way. She was determined to show that she could make it in the top division and play a part in Barcelona's success.

Soon, Aitana's effort and patience paid off, and she was rewarded with her Barcelona debut. It was in the domestic competition, the Copa de la Reina. Barcelona had been drawn against Real Sociedad, a top division team from the Basque country. Aitana didn't get herself on the score sheet, but she certainly made an impact for her team. She showed endless energy and enthusiasm in the middle of the pitch, making sure her opponents rarely got a chance on the ball. Aitana also showed off her attacking qualities, providing an assist for Bárbara Latorre late in the game to help rubber stamp Barcelona's authority on the match.

With Aitana's help, Barcelona won and progressed to the next round of the cup with a 1-5 victory.

AITANA BONMATÍ

Aitana was also included in the squad for another cup competition that season, helping Barcelona on their way to the final of the Copa Catalunya – a local tournament made up of teams from the region of Catalonia. Barcelona were the strongest team in the region, and usually won the tournament, but Aitana knew this was no time to take it easy. She gave the competition everything she had, resulting in a firm 6-0 victory against RCD Espanyol in the final of the competition. A proud Aitana had won her first ever women's trophy with the Barcelona first team. It might not have been a league title, or even the Copa de le Reina, but it was a competition that meant a lot to the fans and meant that Barcelona had proved yet again that they were the best team in Catalonia.

Aitana was occasionally picked during the club's 2016/2017 Liga F campaign. She made thirteen appearances and even scored two goals when Barcelona demolished Oiartzun 13-0 towards the end of the season. Unfortunately, Barcelona finished as runners up by three points behind Atlético de Madrid.

It had been another frustrating year for Barcelona and for Aitana. The team had the determination and the talent to win, but they had been unable to achieve their goals. Aitana would have loved the opportunity to play more of a part on the pitch, though she understood that it was going to take time and that she needed to keep on pushing. Aitana wanted nothing more than to play every week, wearing the blue and garnet stripes of the Barcelona shirt with pride.

CAPTAIN BONMATÍ

Aitana's rise to the first team of Barcelona had not gone unnoticed by the national team. She continued to be called up to represent her country in youth tournaments and was announced in the squad for Spain's U19 Euro campaign, a summer tournament being held in Northern Ireland.

The Spanish U19 team had competed in three consecutive final defeats in this competition. With Aitana on board, the team hoped that they could put an end to this tournament's curse. But due to Aitana's forceful personality, Spain were going to have to play the first few matches without her ...

The midfielder had been given a three-game ban after picking up a straight red card in a qualifying match against Belgium. Aitana's fierceness and dedication usually worked in her favour. However, in this match, she overstepped the mark and was sent off the pitch and given the ban as a punishment for her behaviour. Aitana was disappointed not to be able to play, but she understood that her actions had consequences, and she had every faith in her team. She knew that her teammates were more than capable of stepping up in her absence, to help push Spain through to the next round of the tournament.

Spain had been drawn in

Group A and would play against Germany, Scotland and Northern Ireland. The team's competition got off to a strong start with a 0-2 victory against Northern Ireland. But they hit a stumbling block and were defeated in their next match against Germany, losing the game 2-0. This meant that Spain needed to win their third game if they were to emerge from the group stages. With Aitana cheering on her team from the sidelines they did exactly that. Spain defeated Scotland 1-0 and secured their spot in the knock-out rounds of the competition.

Even better, Aitana had now served her three-game suspension, so she would finally be able to have an impact on the tournament.

But before she could get back onto the pitch, the Spanish team's manager had some news for her. Aitana was returning to the team as captain. The manager saw her as someone who the rest of the squad could look up to. They believed she was a natural-born leader who had the ability to help push this team all the way to the end of the tournament.

AITANA BONMATÍ

Spain faced off against the Netherlands in a fiercely fought semi-final. But with Aitana back, the Spanish team were able to carry the day. Spain won the match 3-2, earning themselves a spot in the final. Now they just had to overcome an incredibly talented French side in order to win the tournament. Aitana and the rest of the team were very aware that France had defeated Spain in the 2016 final of this competition. The players couldn't help but think about their so-called tournament curse. This was the exact stage where the team had failed previously three times in a row, and they were determined not to let it happen again. After all, there was too much talent and heart in the Spanish team to let superstition take hold. It was time for the Spain U19 team to break the curse.

The French struck first in the final, with Mathilde Bourdieu scoring in the 4th minute of the match. But Spain refused to allow this early set back to define the match. Patricia Guijarro, a Barcelona teammate of Aitana, scored an equaliser in the

18th minute. The game was level again and there everything was there to play for.

The rest of the match turned into a difficult back-and-forth tie. Both sides desperately tried and failed to find the elusive winning goal. Then, with less than twenty minutes to go, one side finally broke the deadlock. Emelyne Laurent found the back of the net for France in the 71st minute. This gave France an all-important 2-1 lead, especially when there wasn't much time left in the game. One of the Spanish defenders booted the ball away in frustration. Looking around, Aitana could see the same frustration written over the rest of her teammates' faces. She knew that she needed to act fast in order to save the game. As captain, it was her responsibility to keep everyone's energy high. She quickly rallied the team, letting them know that she believed in each and every one of them and that there was still time to get out there and win. Spain pushed and pushed, but despite their best efforts they just couldn't seem to find that goal.

But finally, in the 85th minute, the Spanish team proved that the game really wasn't over until the final whistle. Damaris Egurrola, a Spanish midfielder, grabbed her opportunity after the ball was launched into the penalty area. Egurrola knew she had one shot and gave it everything she had. Both teams held their breath as the ball flew past the outstretched hands of the French goalkeeper, Myléne Chavas, and straight into the goal. As Egurrola celebrated, the rest of the team couldn't contain their joy.

They had found their way back into the game, and still had a chance at winning the competition.

The match took another turn in the 87th minute. Pauline Dechilly, a French defender, took a free kick before the referee had blown the whistle. By the rules of the game this was a yellow card, but as Dechilly had already been given a yellow card earlier in the match, she was sent off. The French defender left the pitch in tears, leaving the French team with only ten players for the rest of the game.

AITANA BONMATÍ

Time was running out.

In the 90th minute, Spain earned themselves a free kick. The ball swung into the penalty box and was met with a header by Guijarro. The ball flew into the back of the net. Guijarro had scored and Spain were in the lead. Aitana and the rest of the Spanish team piled on top of their teammate in celebration. They could hardly believe it. They were actually winning. Could the tournament curse finally be broken?

There were only a few minutes left

in the match, but for Aitana and the rest of the team it felt like a lifetime before the referee finally blew the whistle. Every single member of the Spanish staff and the rest of the squad ran onto the pitch to join in with the celebration.

Aitana had one more responsibility as captain: to collect the trophy. She walked proudly over to her teammates on the winner's podium, a golden medal around her neck.

Aitana paused for a moment and allowed the fans' cheers to rise. With a massive grin

AITANA BONMATÍ

on her face, she lifted the trophy in the air. Spain were the champions at last!

9
LA BLAUGRANA

On the back of her successful international tournament, Aitana couldn't help but feel hopeful about the future. She wanted to carry the momentum with her into her club football and make sure she earned more match time on the pitch. But

AITANA BONMATÍ

as she had already learnt, the world of football is hugely competitive, and in a team already crammed with talent even cup winners didn't always make the team.

To Aitana's disappointment, she featured sparingly for Barcelona during their 2017/2018 season. Although she picked up more appearances than the previous year, she often spent matchdays on the sideline.

It wasn't all bad though. Aitana scored her first Champions League goal that year in a match against FC Gintra, a team from Lithuania. And Aitana was also given a substitute appearance in the 2018 Copa de la Reina final, when she was brought into the game in the second half. The match was locked at 0-0. Neither side had been able to find a goal in ninety minutes, so the game had to be settled in extra time. In the final few seconds, Barcelona's Mariona Caldentey scored, causing the fans watching to game to erupt into cheers and the players to run riot on the pitch. Barcelona won the Copa de la

AITANA BONMATÍ

Reina thanks to that last gasp winner, and Aitana was happy to know she had played a part. But she wanted much more for her career. Aitana wanted to play each and every match. To do this, she knew she had to improve and develop to a point where the manager felt they had no choice but to include her.

Aitana did everything she could to build up her skills, putting in hours and hours of extra practice. Her hard work, determination and single-mindedness paid off in the 2018/2019 campaign.

The coaches had seen the work that she put in, and finally believed that Aitana was ready to become an integral part of the team.

Aitana made thirty-seven appearances for the team across all competitions – only missing out on five matches all season! And Aitana proved their confidence in her was deserved. She scored thirteen goals over the season and played a crucial role in Barcelona's Liga F, Copa de la Reina and Champions League efforts. The team finished as runners up in

★ AITANA BONMATÍ ★

Liga F, made it to the semi-finals of the Copa de la Reina and even into the final of that year's Champions League in Budapest. They knew the final was going to be tough; Barcelona were facing against an incredibly talented Lyon side in Budapest.

Sadly, the final left Aitana and Barcelona's dream of winning in tatters. The French side proved unstoppable, putting four goals past Barcelona in the opening thirty minutes. Barcelona's Asisat Oshoala scored a late defiant goal for her team, but it just wasn't enough. To the Spanish side's disappointment, Lyon were crowned as the winners of the Champions League. But the team rightly took a lot of pride in making it that far in the tournament – they had been only ninety minutes away from being crowned as the best women's football team in Europe. Despite this, Aitana was crushed. She hated being so close to winning but not returning home with the trophy. She decided there and then that she wasn't going to let herself, her team or the fans experience this feeling again.

10
NATIONAL TEAM

While Aitana had become a frequent starter for Barcelona, she had also been picking up more appearances for Spain. Aitana was regularly called up to national team squads for friendlies and qualifying fixtures.

Aitana's first goal for her country

★ **FOOTBALL RISING STARS** ★

was during a friendly against England. It was a warm-up match that had been organised for both sides to prepare for the upcoming 2019 World Cup. Aitana was over the moon, but she had her eye on an even bigger goal. With the tournament fast approaching, it was time for the Spanish coach, Jorge Vilda, to pick his squad for the tournament. Aitana hoped she had done enough to earn a spot but she couldn't be certain.

After all, the country was filled with talented players and every spot would be hotly contested. There was nothing she could do except wait and hope for the announcement, which was to be made in a few weeks' time.

Those weeks felt like years to Aitana, but finally it was time for the announcement. When Aitana heard her name, she could hardly contain herself! She had actually done it – she would be taking part in her first ever major international competition. Everything she had dreamt of and worked for was finally coming true. She knew that playing in a women's tournament would be something entirely different from the youth levels she had been in before. But it was a challenge that Aitana couldn't wait to rise to.

Aitana and the rest of the squad travelled to France for the tournament. Aitana was too excited to dwell on her fear of flying this time. Before she knew it, she was settling into her accommodation with the rest of the team, and it was time to focus on their opponents. Spain had been placed against South Africa, Germany and China in Group B. They knew if they worked hard and gave it everything they had, they had every chance of progressing to the next stage. Spain's first match of the tournament was against South Africa at Stade Océane in Le Havre. Spain were favourites for the match, but South Africa were not going to walk away without a fight. The underdogs scored the first goal of the match in the 25th minute, as Thembi Kgatlana fired in an impressive long-range strike, giving South Africa a 1-0 lead. Aitana was a substitute for the game and could do nothing but watch helplessly from the bench as the ball flew into the net. Spain desperately tried to find an equaliser in the first half, but South Africa held them off.

Vilda knew that he needed to freshen up the team and made two substitutions at half-time. The manager decided to bring Lucía García and an excited Aitana into the team for the second half. Aitana, and the the rest of the team, kept pushing for an equaliser, but it wasn't easy. Finally, however, gaps began to appear in the match. While South Africa's effort and enthusiasm had gotten them into the lead, they were starting to tire. The fitness, technical ability and style of Spanish football was now on show as the team kept pressing forward.

In the 70th minute, Spain were awarded a penalty. Hermoso stepped forward and shot the ball into the net. The match was now level. Then, in the 83rd minute, Spain were awarded another penalty. Things were about to get worse for South Africa.

Nothando Vilakazi was the defender who had made the challenge and received her second yellow card, resulting in a red card, and had to leave the game. This gave Spain the chance to take the lead. Hermoso stepped forward again and effortlessly netted her second penalty. Aitana's fellow substitute, García, put the icing on the cake with a third for the team in the final few minutes of the match. The coach's substitutions had worked, and Spain had avoided losing the opening match. Aitana was proud of her performance in the game and most importantly of how she had helped her country earn three precious points.

But the second group match did not go as Spain hoped. The team fell to a 1-0 defeat against Germany. Spain played well in the match, and Aitana made a brief appearance as a substitute, but Germany's goal from Sara Däbritz was enough to win the match. However, everything wasn't lost. Spain played out a 0-0 draw against China in the final game of the group, which earned the team a spot in the round of 16. Spain would be playing against the USA. Aitana and Spain could not have wished for a worse draw. The USA were previous winners of the tournament and were the team expected to triumph once again. To make it any further in the competition, Spain would have to defeat the favourites.

The two sides battled for progression inside the Stade Auguste-Delaune in Reims. The US struck the first blow, as Megan Rapinoe fired her team into the lead with a penalty in the 7th minute. But Spain refused to admit defeat. Two minutes later, Hermoso took advantage of some poor defending from the American side and levelled the game in the 9th minute. After a fast-paced start, the game moved into an even rhythm. Both sides fought to take the lead but neither were able to do so. This pattern continued into the second half until a controversial but decisive moment. The USA's Rose Lavelle took the ball down in the box and pushed it in front of her. Virginia Torrecilla, the Spanish defender, tried to tackle her and her studs grazed the shin pads of Lavelle. Feeling the contact, the attacker fell to the ground with her arms raised. The referee saw the incident and immediately pointed to the penalty spot. Sitting on the substitutes bench, Aitana and the entire Spanish team couldn't believe it. As far as they were concerned it shouldn't be a penalty. The referee was recommended to view the incident on the pitch-side monitor – something that's usually suggested for referees to do when the accompanying VAR officials believe an error may have been made. The referee watched the footage but stood by her decision, leaving the Spanish team and fans upset, confused and angry. Rapinoe comfortably tucked away the penalty and the US were 2-1 in the lead. All Aitana could do was watch, and hope, that her teammates could come back from the brink. Spain gave it everything they had, but the match finished 2-1. Spain were knocked out of the tournament.

Aitana was crushed, but as the days passed that feeling lessened and she slowly realised just how proud of herself she was. She had played in a World Cup! And for every single minute she had spent on the pitch, Aitana had done her best to make her country proud. This tournament might not have gone exactly how she had hoped, but she was still a young football player. If she continued to develop and excel, there would be more opportunities waiting for her. There would be more matches, competitions and opportunities to play for her country on the international stage. She would be able to play

AITANA BONMATÍ

a bigger part and maybe help her country to win a major international trophy during her career.

LIGA F

Aitana returned to Barcelona and continued to play exceptionally for her club during the 2019/2020 season. But it turned out to be a year unlike any other, as the world was brought to a halt by the COVID-19 pandemic. The football season had to stop, and the decision was made

that the campaign would have to be abandoned. Due to their position in the table, and expected points, Barcelona were awarded the league title that year. Aitana had her first ever Liga F triumph, but it was a bittersweet victory – she would have much preferred to win a title by actually playing. But of course she and every other player understood that there were far bigger things than football to worry about.

Eventually, football started again, and Barcelona and Aitana enjoyed an unforgettable 2020/2021 campaign.

With Aitana's help, Barcelona were crowned as champions in Liga F two years in a row. The team stormed their way to first position in the league by winning an astonishing thirty-three matches out of a total of thirty-four. The team won the league by an impressive twenty-five point margin and wrapped up the title with plenty of matches to spare. Aitana had earned another Liga F triumph, but this one was far sweeter. This time, she felt that she and Barcelona had truly earned the title of champions. The team had also progressed well into the Champions League and the Copa de la Reina. Could they win those too? Aitana started to think the almost unthinkable. Could Barcelona become the first ever Spanish women's football club to complete a continental treble?

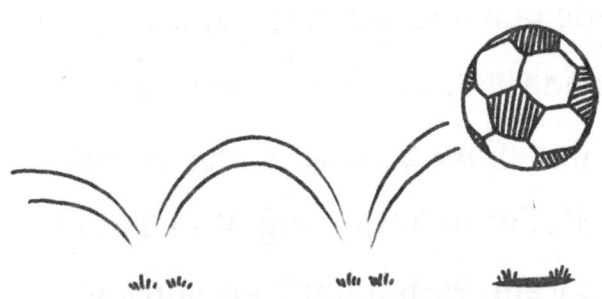

12
THE TREBLE

Having added one trophy to the cabinet, it was time to fight for the second. Thanks to a determined and talented run, Barcelona had made it all the way to the final of the Champions League. Victories against PSV, Fortuna Hjørring, Manchester City and Paris Saint-Germain had set up a final clash against Chelsea. Both teams ferociously wanted to claim victory in the final.

The two sides met at the Gamla Ullevi in Gothenburg, a football stadium in the second largest city of Sweden. The tension on the pitch was heightened because there were no fans in attendance due to the after-effects of COVID-19. But this didn't make the match any less important. The stage was set, the trophy was waiting, and the glory was within touching distance.

Only thirty-three seconds

into the match, Barcelona took the lead in the most unusual manner. The team applied pressure in their opponent's box, and everyone was scrambling. Chelsea's Fran Kirby tried to clear the ball, but her effort struck the shin of her teammate, Melanie Leupolz. The ball, moving with speed, looped towards the goal and over Ann-Katrin Berger in the Chelsea net. Barcelona had the lead! It was a nightmare start for Chelsea, but a dream for Barcelona.

Chelsea tried to strike back immediately. Pernille

AITANA BONMATÍ

Harder, Chelsea's striker, ran into the box unmarked and prodded the ball towards goal. Her effort flew just inches over the crossbar, leaving Barcelona still in the lead.

Confidence oozed from the Barcelona side. There was a smile on every player's face as they realised that they really could do this. The pressure and weight of expectation was lifted from their shoulders and replaced with simple joy and excitement.

Barcelona scored a second goal in the 14th minute. Putellas placed the ball into the centre of the goal as the goalkeeper dived to her left, unable to do anything as the ball hit the back of the net.

Barcelona were far from finished. They knew there were still goals to be scored, and they were determined to do so. In the 20th minute, it was Aitana's turn to shine. Barcelona's Lieke Martens made a dangerous run down the left wing, crossing the ball into the box. Hermoso brought it under her control with her back to the goal, then passed it to Putellas,

who played a beautiful one touch pass forward to Aitana in the box. Aitana wriggled past the remaining defender and struck the ball into the goal with her left boot. As the thwack echoed around the empty stadium, Aitana sprinted out of the box with her arms outstretched while her teammates cheered. They had a 0-3 lead in the opening twenty minutes of the match. They could not have dreamt of a better start and were loving every moment.

Caroline Graham Hansen added a fourth for Barcelona in the 36th minute, and it was clear that the game was completely under their control from that moment on. Chelsea fought bravely for the remainder of the match, but no more goals were scored.

After the referee blew her whistle, Barcelona were officially the champions of the 2020/2021 Champions League. Aitana fell to the ground with her body outstretched and took in the moment. She had just helped her team achieve the highest honour in club football. She didn't think it was possible to feel any happier as Barcelona's captain, Losada, lifted the trophy. The club had officially secured their second trophy of the season. And there was still a chance that this campaign could get even better. It was only a matter of weeks before Barcelona played in the Copa de le Reina final.

As Barcelona's third final of the season approached, the team focussed everything they had on the upcoming match. This was their chance to achieve the continental treble. It was something that had never before been achieved by a Spanish women's team.

Barcelona were facing Levante in the final. Their opponents tried their best, but no one could stop Barcelona in their current form. They were unstoppable. An ecstatic Barcelona won the match 4-2, writing themselves into the history books as one of the best ever Spanish women's football teams. Aitana wasn't just an incredibly talented player on the world stage for Barcelona, she had cemented herself as a footballing legend. Her name would always be remembered as a part of the mesmerising team that dominated women's football in the 2020/2021 season.

13
EURO 2022

Aitana and Barcelona continued building their success in the 2021/2022 season. They accomplished a domestic treble by winning Liga F, Copa de la Reina and the Supercopa de España.

But as the club football season ended, Aitana had no time to relax or reflect on how far she had come. She had been named as part of the Spanish squad and was headed straight to England to compete for the Euro 2022 trophy. Spain were not the favourites to win, especially because they had been hit by a heavy blow before the start of the tournament. Aitana's Barcelona teammate, Putellas, had suffered a painful injury that would keep her away from the pitch for a substantial amount of time. This meant the Spanish team were missing one of their best players. But as every player knew, football was never about the individual, it was about the team. Spain still had a chance at winning if everyone came together and performed. There was no doubt that they were a talented team, and they were more than capable of challenging any side they came up against.

Spain had been drawn in Group B and would play against Finland, Germany and Denmark. This was a difficult group, but Aitana believed they could triumph.

★ AITANA BONMATÍ ★

Spain's first opponents were Finland. The Spanish side began their competition as they meant to go on. The team defeated their opponents 4-1. Aitana even got herself on the score sheet with a goal in the 41st minute of the match, helping her team achieve three points.

In the second match against Germany, they were defeated 2-0, but they were able to get out of the group thanks to a 1-0 win against Denmark. This match was not an easy win and Spain only progressed thanks to a

90th minute winner scored by Marta Cardona, meaning the team were through to the knock-out rounds.

Just like the draw for the 2019 World Cup, the draw for Euro 2022 wasn't favourable for Spain. They would need to defeat England to make it past the quarter-finals. England was hosting the tournament, which meant the stands were packed with thousands of supportive and roaring English fans. But Aitana and her teammates believed in their talent and skill, as did the Spanish fans. They were a fantastic team and there was no way they were going to roll over without a fight. Aitana and her teammates were going to do their best to ruin England's party.

The match took place at the home of Brighton & Hove Albion in front of 28,944 fans – with the majority of the crowd in the stadium cheering for England. Aitana and her teammates walked out into a hostile environment. But they had a gameplan, determination and a quiet confidence that they had what it took to win.

England had strolled through the group stages of the tournament, but it quickly became apparent that their stroll had come to an end. The two sides played out a nervous first half with neither side able to find the net. But in the second half, in the 54th minute, the stadium was suddenly silent. Spain's Athenea del Castillo sprinted down the right wing and found Esther González in the centre of the box. The striker fired the ball into the net and gave Spain a 0-1 lead. The players' shouts of celebration echoed around the stands as the

AITANA BONMATÍ

English fans watched in stunned silence. Could it be that Spain were on their way to knocking the hosts out of the tournament? Aitana and her teammates defended their lead bravely, but as time started to run out England created a chance. In the 84th minute, Alessia Russo won a header in the box and the ball fell to Ella Toone, who scored. The match was now level. Aitana and the rest of the Spanish team had to pick themselves up, knowing that anything could happen in the next few minutes.

Regular time ended at 1-1, so the match went into extra time. In the end, a moment of individual brilliance defined the game. In the 95th minute, England's Georgia Stanway fired a long-distance rocket towards the goal, and the Spanish goalkeeper, Pānos, was unable to stop it. Stanway scored and Spain were unable to reply. Extra time ended and England were through to the semi-final. Aitana and Spain had been knocked out of the tournament.

Aitana was disappointed, but she was also proud of how hard her team had fought. They had come so close to winning and causing one of the shocks of the tournament. But it just wasn't to be at Euro 2022. Aitana had been picking up trophies at Barcelona like pick 'n' mix sweets, but her first major international trophy with the women's team still evaded her. She was determined not to see it as a failure or a disappointment. Instead, it was another challenge that Aitana could not wait to fight for.

14
CAMPIONES!

As the summer of 2023 begins, Aitana is taking a well-deserved break. It's not only a chance for her to recharge her batteries but to also look back on her incredible success. She has come a long way from the young girl playing football on the streets of Sant Pere de Ribes. She is

AITANA BONMATÍ

now an integral part of Barcelona's history, present and future.

Aitana has recently added to her ever-growing trophy collection. She helped lead Barcelona to the Liga F title during the 2022/2023 season. The men's team also won La Liga in the same year, making the campaign an unforgettable one for Barcelona as a club.

Aitana also helped her team win the club's second Champions League trophy. She displayed her usual grit and desire on one of the world's biggest stages, as Barcelona triumphed over Wolfsburg 3-2 in the final. The team had been losing the match 0-2 at halftime, but they came back in the second half to score three goals and bring the trophy home to Catalonia. To add the cherry on top, Aitana was given the player of the season award for her efforts during the Champions League campaign.

Aitana has now achieved almost everything that it is possible to achieve with Barcelona. But her

numerous medals and victories haven't dampened her passion

or her desire to win. Every single time she puts on the Barcelona shirt she is determined to play with the same spirit and desire as she did when she first made her debut. Back then, she worked tirelessly day after day to earn her break in the Barcelona academy, and she still works every bit as hard today, determined to make her fans proud. She is a player who truly deserves to wear the shirt and always gives her all to every performance and match.

# ★ FOOTBALL RISING STARS ★

Aitana carried her form with her into the international break. She joined up with her teammates to play her part in an inspirational 2023 World Cup. The co-hosts of the tournament, Australia and New Zealand, could not have predicted the Spanish masterclass that was about to sweep their shores.

Though they were not the favourites for the tournament, Aitana and her country proved any doubters wrong by not only making it to the final, but by winning the entire competition! For the first time ever, Aitana helped lead her country to a major international women's trophy, outperforming a strong England team in the final of the competition thanks to their skill, ability and star players. Everyone played at their best when they needed to, and they did it all with a touch of admirable flair.

Aitana has enjoyed many successes with Barcelona, winning countless trophies and making incredible moments happen. And once more she has turned football into art with her midfield displays, demonstrating just how powerful and successful a girl from Catalonia can be on the global stage.

The current Barcelona women's team number 14 is also an ambassador for the Johan Cruyff Foundation. Aitana was the first woman in 2021 to sponsor a Cruyff Court – one of the foundation's free-to-use small soccer fields to encourage sports among young  people in Sitges. She also works with the United Nations' Refugee Agency.

AITANA BONMATÍ

And it is this work that allows her to keep fighting for what she believes is right.

Only a handful of years ago, she was a young girl making her way to the front of a crowd to watch Barcelona on a small TV screen – one of many in Sant Pere de Ribes who lived and breathed football. Supporting her heroes whenever she could and dreaming of wearing the blue and garnet of Barcelona. And today she is doing exactly that. She's no longer a fan in the crowd but the star player on the pitch.

★ FOOTBALL RISING STARS ★

She is the hero thousands of young girls and boys across the world look up to, wishing that one day they can be like Aitana Bonmatí Conca.